An impossible request leads to death, but is it the right thing to do?

"Gotta do it fast," Mary said. "Like Al Pacino in the first Godfather movie when he shoots the gangster and the dirty cop."

Harry and I had forgone the usual PI baggy suits and ties, instead preferring to don jeans and tee shirts. In addition I had added a New York Yankees ball cap and mirrored sunglasses. Harry, the Mr. GQ of our little firm, hated the disguises, but it would lessen the chances of being identified.

As I sat in the Impala I felt my stomach churn. A trace of bile invaded my mouth when I spotted the very much alive Mary O'Shay coming down the sidewalk toward me.

She looked happy. Doubt nearly forced me from the car to warn her about the other guy. But a greater fear of my own failure kept me glued to the seat. Harry said the accident was going to happen no matter what I did.

Mary would either die or be in a coma. What kind of choices were these? Why couldn't I just hit the guy who would hit her, and save her from the coma?

Harry said the only thing we could change was the time of Mary's accident, not the inevitability of it.

Tales of **Weird** Fantasy

Russ Crossley

Published by 53rd Street Publishing
www.53rdstreetpublising.com

Tales of **Weird** Fantasy

Published by 53rd Street Publishing
Copyright 2011 Russ Crossley
All rights reserved

Cover image © Myfairies | Dreamstime.com

ISBN trade paperback edition 978-1-927621-24-0

Dedication

For Rita, my best friend who's unconditional love
makes life worth living.

.

Table of Contents

Introduction

In this collection of stories you will discover magical swords with unfathomable power, ghosts, the future of crime, an alternate universe where the royalty of Europe's power never waned until the 21st century, and meet the children of fictions most iconic monster.

These tales are diverse and weird, but each conveys a message of hope and/or warning that we humans are as diverse as the world we live in.

I hope you enjoy these five tales as much as I enjoyed creating them. As always if you have any feedback please contact me via Facebook, Twitter, or one of my websites.

Only The Worthy

SYDNEY GIDEON WASN'T GOING to be happy his foreman had ignored his orders not to open the thousand-year-old stone sarcophagus. Sure, the man wanted to remove the White-Hilt from its long hidden resting place by himself. But from what Nick had heard Gideon didn't trust anyone. Not even his foot solders. This disaster would only serve to reinforce the leader of the Brother's paranoid delusions.

Why are billionaire's always such nut jobs?

Nick Sparta engaged the filter on his auto-focus binoculars just as the sphere of brilliant golden flame began to consume the excavation site. He watched the white-hot fire render the flesh from the bones of the excavation crew as it swept over them. The massive excavator melted into slag, as did other smaller work vehicles scattered around the site.

A growling, fierce wall of death enveloped men and equipment so fast there was no chance for them to escape, or even time to scream. The flames were like a ravenous beast in search of fresh prey. Everyone within half a mile of the sword was now charred into dust, but at least their deaths had been swift.

"Small mercies," Nick murmured under his breath. He scanned the devastation with the binoculars looking for any signs of life and found none.

No doubt in the last millisecond of his life the foreman must have realized he should have waited for the Priests of the Brotherhood. The foreman would have no second chance to misjudge matters. "Greed so often courts disaster," Nick sighed.

Nick hoped his own life wouldn't end that way — in a flaming nightmare resulting from his own stupidity.

From his camouflaged listening post, hidden amongst boulders the size of bungalows, over a mile from ground zero, Nick shrugged.

Poor bastards, he thought. But better them than me.

When you're in the world-domination business you have to expect collateral damage. Gideon certainly did.

The white-hot flame dissipated into the cold air. This was accompanied by the crackle of static discharge. It didn't take long for the damp Queen Charlotte Island winds to return to send a chill through his all weather gear after the wave of superheated air had passed over him.

He consoled himself with the thought that the icy rain had finally given way to a constant drizzle. For the past three weeks he'd been camped out on this wind-and-rain swept island to observe the Brotherhoods retrieval operation. Not even hot coffee warmed his insides anymore

Just as he was about to give up hope of finding anyone alive he spotted someone at the edge of his field of vision. He lay face down on the beach. His head-to-foot black clothing contrasted against the grey sand beach. Anywhere else in the world the smooth sandy beach would be an ideal tourist spot. As the weather in the Haida Gwaii archipelago was not conducive to sun worshipers it meant there was a good chance the survivor wasn't a tourist.

In the dim light Nick thumbed the button to remove the filter. The contrast sharpened and he engaged the zoom feature to focus on the unmoving body. If the man was alive he was the lone survivor of the wrath of the Dyrnwyn.

According to Welsh legend the magical sword had once belonged to Rhydderch Hael, one of the Three Generous Men of Britain. The old tales said that when an unworthy man drew the Dyrnwyn, or White Hilt, from its scabbard he would burn. If drawn by a worthy man the fire from the White Hilt would aid him in his rightful cause. Given today's events, it would seem the legend contained more truth than most. Problem was what cause would an ancient magical sword consider worthy?

The good news for the Brotherhood was that this part of the Charlottes was about as remote an area on Earth as it got. This meant the destruction of the local ecosystem would go unnoticed — at least for a while. Nick doubted if any of the government owned spy satellites were tasked to scrutinize this heap of volcanic rock in the North Pacific. There were no tactical assets of interest to the world powers in these islands. Except now, with the release of this much electro-magnetic discharge, he expected the level of interest by the world powers was about to rise. And quickly. Time was short. He needed to make a sat-call.

He set the binoculars down and peered into the mist. The twitching survivor was about two thousand yards from his position. A frown creased Nick's tanned forehead.

The Brotherhood's support vessel, with its helicopter, still rode the waves offshore. Since the chopper hadn't lifted off yet he might have time. If he could get to the survivor before the rescuers came, he might have the lead he needed to find out where the Brotherhood planned to take the sword, and what they planned to do with it.

Given past history both he and his employer suspected the Brotherhood's worldwide search for the Thirteen Treasures of Britain was the precursor to a much larger scheme. His mission was to find out what they were planning and, if need be, find a way to stop them. If he failed his employer would be forced to play the nuclear card. It could mean a lot of collateral damage.

He made his decision.

He shoved the binoculars into the holster on his belt. He then slipped out from behind the camouflage screen and began to pick his way across the rocks. His boots and gloves were designed to grip ice so he was able to move as fast as the local wildlife across the slick seaweed-coated rocks.

Nick kept his profile as low as possible as he moved toward the beach. His brown eyes flitted in the direction of the support vessel.

Though visible through the mist, he thought he saw the rotor blades on the helicopter begin to turn. He felt his abs tighten.

If the Brotherhood discovered him here he was dead. Section N had lost three agents in the past three years attempting to get close to the Brotherhood's operations. He was the only one who'd managed to get this far. In fact, he was the only one still alive. And he wanted to stay alive at least as much as he wanted to track the bastards down.

If he messed up the mission would be compromised. His gut told him failure was not an option. The clock was ticking, and Nick had been at this game far too long not to listen to his gut.

Time to move faster.

He stepped onto the sand just as the sky began to brighten. He could see the black clouds were clearing in the east. He estimated it would be dawn in less than half an hour. While his stealth suit was good, he knew he could be seen against the contrast of the sand, in the light of day.

He figured his chances of succeeding before the helicopter arrived were at nine point two-seven percent.

He would barely have time to retrieve the survivor, if he was in any shape to talk, and get back under cover, before retreating to his listening post. The sword would have to wait.

He glanced at the support ship and saw the black shape of the helicopter lift into the air.

He ran for the target.

Nick estimated there was a thousand yards between him and the survivor. He closed the distance fast.

Nick dropped to his knees in the wet sand beside the still form. Still breathing —good. Nick grabbed the guy's thin arms and heaved the body over his shoulders.

The guy's lighter than I expected.

Nick ran for cover. His breath came in gasps.

He stole a quick glance in the direction of the inbound helicopter. He saw it was headed for the still smoking excavation site, not for the beach. His odds of not being spotted had just improved.

Nick finally reached the cover of the boulders. He moved to a spot out of line of sight with the beach. He slipped the limp body off his shoulders and placed him on the ground, the guy's back against a massive boulder.

The man's head slumped to his chest and his arms hung loose at his sides. He was dressed in a chocolate brown winter parka with brown fur around the hood, hiking boots, waterproof pants, and thick winter gloves. A navy blue balaclava hid his face.

For all Nick knew, it could be Santa Claus in there under all those clothes

Nick sat down on his haunches next to his charge and hung his head. He took several depth breaths, letting his heart rate return to normal.

He rose to his feet to peek around the boulder. The helicopter had landed a few yards shy of the destroyed excavation site. It didn't look like they'd seen him. Just to be on the safe side he had to get back to his camouflaged listening post.

He turned back to study the survivor. He was slim, probably weighted no more than a hundred and twenty-five pounds, medium height, about five nine or so, with smallish hands.

The survivor was a woman.

"This could be interesting," Nick said.

He removed the balaclava from her head. As he did shoulder length, hair the color of copper wire, spilled onto her narrow shoulders. She wasn't a model beauty, but certainly pretty. Her skin was pale.

Her rosy cheeks bore the orange freckles common of true redheads. She was breathing.

Score one for the good guys.

He reached for the canteen he kept attached to the tool belt around his waist. After the cap was removed he raised her head and, after taking a sip to moisten his own dry mouth, splashed cold water on her face. She moaned softly and her eyes opened to slits. "Uhhh," she murmured. She threw her head back and it struck the rock. "Owww."

Her left hand went to the spot where her head had contacted the stone. "Where am I?" she said as she rubbed the back of her head.

"Same place you were before. The Charlottes," said Nick. He imagined after the explosion and striking the rock she must have the worst headache since Moses brought the plagues to the Pharaoh. He smirked.

The woman glared at him. "What's so funny?"

"Nothing. Just a little dark humor is all." Nick shrugged. "Sorry, it's a weakness in my line of work."

She nodded. "Owww. It's not funny."

"Yeah. I agree. Can you stand?"

"Yes, I think so." He held her hand then gripped her arm in his other hand to help steady her. She stood slowly; using the smooth boulder rock as a backstop.

"I'm sorry about this, but we have to get off the beach and back to my listening post." He nodded toward the group of four men who had disembarked from the helicopter. They were headed for the stone sarcophagus at the epicenter of the blackened sand and earth.

The woman squinted at the scene and her rosy cheeks paled. "We have to stop them," she said then teetered. One hand went to her forehead. Her eyes closed. She almost fell until Nick wrapped one muscular arm around her narrow waist. He then carried her limp body across the rocky landscape.

***

Once behind the stealth shield Nick set his new charge on his single padded camp chair. He sat across from her on a rock.

He removed the form-fitted hood of his stealth suit and gasped for breath. The suit was effective for surveillance operations, but it was too warm for running cross-country with a hundred pound weight slung over your shoulder. The designers should add an air conditioner feature.

He blew air from his lungs and then took in several more deep breaths.

After a few moments the woman opened her eyes. "So that's what you look like," she said with a twinkle in her voice. "Not bad."

Nick smiled. "What did you mean when you said we had to stop them? Who is them?"

"Sydney Gideon." Nick looked at her quizzically. "My employer," she continued. "The one after the sword."

Nick shrugged as if he didn't know what she was talking about. She erupted in a mirthless laugh. "The one who nearly killed us." Her expression became sly. "Com'on, Mr...?"

"Nick Sparta."

"Well, Mr. Sparta —"

"Call me Nick."

She nodded. "OK, Nick. My name's Dr. Tiffany Wilson-Tyne by the way — you must be the best equipped tourist in history."

Nick offered a tight-lipped smile. "Oh, just a few comforts from home. You know what they say, never leave home without them."

She looked at the surveillance equipment Section N had provided him.

It included; a directional microphone with a two mile range, a telescopic camera with enough memory for five thousand photographs, an all weather satellite laptop computer powerful enough for use in the Mars Lander, and a satellite phone that allowed him to connect with anywhere on the planet.

Her green eyes lingered on the satellite phone. "Who are you? Really."

Nick smirked. He needed time to think. How did he know he could trust this woman? What was her connection to the White Hilt, and the Brotherhood? Was Sydney Gideon just her employer or was he her Svengali?

"Doctor, huh? Gynecology? Obstetrics?"

She chuckled. "Archaeology actually. Now who are you?" Her tone suggested persistence.

Nick opened the Velcro pouch on his belt and pulled out the faux CIA identification card he carried. He handed it to her.

She looked at it. As she did her lips became a thin line and her brow wrinkled. "CIA? What are you doing here?"

"I should be asking you why an archaeologist is helping the Brotherhood. Whose grave have you robbed? That explosion was rather nasty."

Tiffany sighed and her shoulders slumped. "I know. The idiot foreman shouldn't have touched the sword. I warned him not to touch it, but he ignored me, obviously." She shook her head. "Max wasn't very bright. Though, to be honest, I had no idea the legend of the Dyrnwyn's power was true. After all I'm a scientist not a soothsayer." Her voice carried a hint of regret.

"How did you happen to be on the beach?"

"We were ordered to wait for the priests, so I went for a walk."

Nick doubted she would have left the site of a major archaeological find for the sake of a little exercise.

When the University of British Columbia team announced they'd found an ancient shipwreck on a remote island in the Queen Charlotte chain it had started a firestorm of controversy. Particularly amongst the local aboriginal population, who claimed the vessels remains were of native origin and their property. When it was determined the wreck was a Welsh vessel from pre-history, the academic and scientific community silenced the native protests.

Stone tablets, found in the nearby settlement, told of the exile of a great Welsh King named Owain Dangwyn. Old Welsh legends said he was the last owner of the White Hilt. And the last King to wield the swords power.

The sarcophagus had to be his final resting; the place where the long lost White Hilt was buried.

When the Brotherhood discovered the location of the magic Welsh sword, one of the Thirteen Treasures of ancient Britain, Gideon dispatched his team to retrieve it.

Section N had been monitoring the Brotherhood's ships, planes, and other assets, for months. When their ship sailed, its abrupt departure set off alarm bells.

The satellite net computer model projected the vessel was headed for the northern Canada pacific coast. Satellite surveillance showed the speed the ship traveled meant the vessels turbines were on maximum power for a period longer than they were designed for.

They were in one hell of a hurry and Section N needed to find out why. It was as if someone had poked a wasp's nest with a stick.

Within ten hours Nick was dropped by high altitude Halo parachute jump, to lessen the chance of detection. Within a day of his arrival an unmanned drone submarine delivered the supplies he needed. Once the mission was complete he'd leave the island using the submarine.

The plan was he'd secure the White Hilt, but so far all he'd done was surveillance.

That was until today.

The situation had become more complex.

His job was now to risk manage the changing parameters until his mission objectives were achieved.

The arrival of the woman, which the data models suggested was an acceptable risk, due to her knowledge of Brotherhood operations, was still a wild card in his computations.

"What does the Brotherhood intend to do with the sword and the Thirteen Treasures?"

Tiffany's green eyes narrowed and a look of annoyance flashed through her emerald eyes. She crossed her arms. "Sorry but I signed a confidentiality agreement. I can't discuss it."

Nick stood and stepped toward her. His expression became hard. "Listen, I don't know you very well, but this man Gideon you work for is a very dangerous man. Once your job is done he will kill you."

He was surprised when a smirk replaced her doubtful expression. "Nick, I think that's where you're mistaken. I'm in this for the money. Nothing more. "

Four men, with automatic weapons at the ready, burst through the stealth shield.

Nick knew then he'd been played.

***

The ropes held his arms behind his back.

No matter how he struggled he'd been unable to budge the knots so much as a fraction of a millimeter.

At this rate I'll be free in fifty years. I'll be terminated with extreme prejudice long before then.

After being on land for so long the movement of the ship felt good. The commando-in-charge of the assault had backhanded him during the capture. Nick could still taste the blood in his mouth from the cut in the soft flesh inside his mouth.

He computed the odds of his survival. He estimated his chances were less than five percent. There really was only one option left to him, but it would take the opportune moment to ensure success.

As he was shoved up the ships ladder he caught a glimpse of the helicopter, as it lowered the sarcophagus to the landing pad. He was slammed face first into the freshly painted cold steel wall of the corridor.

Spots clouded his vision as the hulking man grabbed him by his collar and guided him along the narrow corridor. Nick's boots failed to make contact with the deck.

The guard grunted and poked him hard in the kidneys with the barrel of his weapon. Nick winced in pain and stepped into a room.

The room contained a long gray table along one wall, and two armless wooden chairs.

Otherwise it was empty. There wasn't even a porthole.

The guard pushed him toward one of the chairs. The guard used one meaty hand to press him into the chair. He then pulled out a long bladed knife from a holster on his hip.

For a moment, Nick thought the guard was going to kill him. The guard cut the rope from his wrists. It seemed the Brotherhood had other plans for him.

This would be his only chance to escape. The guard stepped back and trained his machine pistol on Nick. "Don't try anything or…" Nick nodded. He understood threats.

After the guard lowered his gun he looped the strap over his left shoulder. He made the mistake of losing eye contact as he moved around the chair. His right hand held a plastic wrist restraint, while his left was wrapped around the machine gun's strap. Nick knew that if the man succeeded in tying him to the chair he was history.

It was time to act.

As the guard moved parallel to Nick's left side, Nick leapt to his feet and head butted him. Stunned by the blow, and already off balance, the guard stumbled away and fell.

He slammed hard face-first into the wall. There was a bone-crushing smack. The impact must've broken the guard's nose because blood squirted over the wall.

Nick moved with inhuman speed to grip the guard's bull-like head in his hands. With a violent jerk of the guards head Nick snapped his neck. Crack.

The guard went limp. He sagged to the floor to land in a heap.

Nick froze as someone behind him applauded.

He turned and saw a robed figure behind him flanked by two more of the burly guards.

"Well done, Mr. Sparta."

"Who's next?" Nick said.

A wicked smile spread over the robed man's chiseled features. He placed his fists on his hips. This parted the priestly robe to reveal the holstered pistol on his right hip, and the hilt of a sword in a scabbard on his left. The two guards raised their machine guns to point them at Nick. "I'm afraid you may well be next, Agent Sparta."

***

The robed priest stood beside the stone sarcophagus. Nick stood near the ships rail flanked by two guards. Seven other armed guards encircled the group.

By now the sun had come out. The warmth of the sunlight felt good on Nick's face after the weeks of rain. The sea air seemed fresher somehow. Seagulls swooped overhead, their cries carried in the gentle breeze that had sprung up. The ship rolled over the ocean swells to dance on its anchor.

Dr. Tiffany stood beside the Priest, her green eyes filled with excitement. She looked like a kid on Christmas morning. Not that Nick had ever experienced Christmas morning.

A crane lifted the stone lid of the sarcophagus into the air and lowered it the deck. Thump.

The Priest of the Brotherhood explained he planned to keep Nick alive for now. Nick would report the successful recovery of the White Hilt by the Brotherhood.

Nick made all the clichéd statements about how mad their plan was, and that Section N wasn't about to standby and let them take over the world, etcetera, but the priest was undeterred.

In fact, he seemed to relish the idea of the nuclear option. He described it as the cleansing. A chance for the world to begin again.

These people are nuts.

"Doctor, I want you to be the first to hold the sacred sword of Rhydderch Hael. Please take it out of the grave."

Tiffany's eyes went wide. "Uhhh...I'm not sure I should. I mean after what happened to Max and the others..." Her lean frame began to tremble even though she still wore the heavy winter parka.

The expressionless eyes of the Priest gazed at her. "Nonsense, Doctor. I want you to have the honor."

Nick realized the priest wanted her to go first. While Nick didn't wish her ill will, he doubted Tiffany Wilson-Tyne was worthy of the swords magic. After all, she was in it for the money.

Nick computed the odds and determined his initial assessment was the only way to stop them now. The survival of the human race was all that mattered.

It was time to act.

Nick grabbed the guard on his left by his wrist. His momentum had caught the man off balance. Nick used the man's weight against him to slide him into another guard.

They fell in a heap of twisting arms and legs. Unable to react in time the other seven guards began to frantically un-slung their weapons.

Before they could level the guns at him, Nick reached into the sarcophagus and had the White Hilt out before anyone could stop him.

Silence. Men frozen with fear. The sound of the breeze and the seagulls, unfazed by the humans' battles.

"No one shoots," the priest warned the guards. They looked at each other in confusion, then lowered their weapons.

"Agent Sparta, you may well be worthy to hold the White Hilt, but only I know how to control its power," the priest said.

He held out his left hand offering to take the ancient sword, while his right moved across his body to grasp the hilt of his own sword. All the priest had to do was shoot Nick and take the sword. But there was no way he could.

Nick knew members of the Brotherhood prided themselves on being experts in the ways of ancient combat. Since Nick had a sword the priest could only use a sword to kill him.

Nick raised the White Hilt until the sharp tip of the gleaming blade was pointed skyward. "It is written that only the worthy may use the Dyrnwyn, provided his cause is just," he said.

"He's right," breathed Tiffany. Her eyes were wide with fear.

She edged back as if she hoped to escape if the flames were to engulf them.

"I must have the sword. It is the destiny of the Brotherhood to possess its power," said the priest.

He drew his sword and charged at Nick. His swarthy features were twisted by rage and determination.

The priest was about to bring his sword's blade down to slice his shoulder when Nick stepped aside and brought the blade of the Dyrnwyn down to strike the priest's skull.

The blade sliced through flesh and bone. The priest emitted a snarl of rage and pain as blood spurted from the mortal wound. But he wasn't done. The priest turned and swung his blade to slice open Nick's right arm from the elbow to the wrist. Blood flowed to the deck.

Flames engulfed the priest's head. The dying man managed to emit a single tortured scream as the flame spread to engulf his body. He collapsed to the deck in a heap of flaming skin and bone.

Nick turned off the pain receptors beneath his artificial skin. He ran for the ships rail. The guards, too stunned by the horror of the priest's death to stop him, watched as Nick vaulted over the ships railing and disappeared.

He landed in the ocean with a splash.

Satellite maps of the seabed showed the support ship was anchored on the edge of an underwater shelf. The shelf on the starboard side of the ship fell away to the deepest trench in the North Pacific. Nick would be buried in the soft silt of the seabed with the sword.

Nick sank until the sunlight was unable to penetrate.

The weight of the sword was sufficient to send him deep into the abyss. He would reach the muddy seabed within a few minutes.

He deactivated his internal locator beacon. He had stopped anyone from possessing the power of the sword. He knew even someone with the best of intentions would be tempted to misuse the power of the Dyrnwyn. For the betterment of mankind the sword must be lost forever.

As Nick sank into the inky blackness he shut down his synaptic pathways. His internal program manager shifted into hibernation mode.

Just before he lost consciousness his artificial intelligence system entered the final stage for safe mode, he felt satisfaction. His mission objectives had been achieved, not exactly as his programmers had planned. Nick Sparta might not continue but the human race would survive, at least for now.

Only the Worthy

In Section N failure was never an option.

Just as it was foretold in the ancient scriptures the White Hilt would once again be in the hands of only the worthy.

A Perfect Crime

BIG PETE SCRATCHED HIS BUTT absentmindedly as he stood in the crowded subway train headed uptown. An elderly lady seated behind him made an ewww noise he ignored.

Teleporters were too expensive on his limited income. He was forced to rely on the squeaking, bone-rattling cattle cars that made up the subway as his transportation of choice (or lack of choice).

These days every subway car was filled to the max with a seething, stinking mass of humanity all day long. The so-called rush-hours of the past were just that, they were in the past.

He smirked. "This here's a condition that's gonna change, and soon," he mused. His fingers tightened around the briefcase's handle in his right hand.

"What's so funny, man?" said a greasy-haired, meghead standing next to him. The puke's sweaty armpit was almost in Pete's face.

He had the appearance of one of those punks who was plugged into a heavy metal I-Pod Implant to listen to his music all day. If you could call that noise music.

Pete preferred the classics; the Stones, Marvin Gaye, Avril Lavagine. Any music was preferable to the junk this kid no doubt listened to twenty-four-seven.

The purple rooster ridge atop the punk's smooth pink head looked like implants. Or maybe his hair had been genetically altered prior to birth. Who knew anymore, and more important why would he care?

"Nuthin' that's any of yore bizness, punk-ass," said Big Pete, his inky gaze traveling up and down the younger man as if he was eyeing a sidewalk turd.

The younger man's eyes shifted to a look of concern. It had obviously dawned on him he had no idea who he was talking to. And while he was a head taller than Big Pete the older man's arms were heavily muscled, and his wide chest stretched his tight dirt-brown tee shirt to reveal the ridges of an equally muscled torso.

Pete fought the urge to chuckle at the guy while he kept his eyes fixed on the younger man's face that was becoming visibly paler with each passing second. Pete always enjoyed the way blood ran from the face of anyone who challenged him.

"Sumthin' wrong?" asked Pete.

The punk shook his head then averted his eyes to stare at the floor of the subway car.

Pete smirked again and went back to thinking about his part in Armand's plan. It was the perfect plan for a perfect crime.

***

Pete arrived outside the Excitement Corporation towers whistling a Stones tune to anyone who had no choice but to listen. He was off key as usual, but he didn't care. Naturally, he failed to notice passersby who lacked an appreciation of his musical talents.

He stopped and gazed upward at the sixty stories of glass and steel tower that housed the world headquarters of the company that was about to define his future. And make him and the others the richest people on the planet.

He entered through a set of revolving glass doors and made his way to the executive elevators to the left of the two identical rows of regular lifts. These were the ones reserved for company executives.

A burly guard, replete with regulation crew cut, and a well-pressed blue and gray uniform, stood with his large muscular arms crossed over his massive chest. His bright blue eyes were fixed on the fireplug-shaped male headed for his position.

Pete saw the slight twitch of the guard's neck muscles. This was the signal to his backup to join him right away.

Good for him, thought Pete. He smells trouble with a capital T when he sees it.

As he arrived in front of the guard a wide smile crossed Pete's swarthy complexion. "Hi."

"Sir." The guard nodded keeping his eyes fixated on Pete. His large hands were folded over each other in front of him as if he were guarding his family jewels. "May I help you," said the guard, the timber of his voice surprisingly high-pitched. His eyes were narrow as Pete watched the man's arms tense, and his booted-feet make those small measured moves to plant himself as if he were a human version of the classic brick wall.

"Big Pete Rustica to see Armand Takly."

The guard's thick dark eyebrows rose slightly upward on his dusky forehead. Pete knew that was because he wasn't the usual class of visitor that visited the Vice-President of Development for the largest Personal Recreational Interface Experience manufacturer in the world. The PRIE was the first and best system ever made.

It was the Blu Ray to the DVD of this generation. Brilliant marketing and a fairly reliable system of making customers dreams come true had made tens of billions of dollars in profits for everyone involved.

Armand Takly had been the chief systems architect of this technological miracle, and rumor was he was about to be arrested on trumped up fraud charges. When he was convicted — and he most certainly would be — his stock options would be revoked. And his bank accounts would be raped, leaving him a penniless pauper rotting in a jail cell.

Not that Armand wasn't guilty.

Every corporate executive was guilty of something. It was just that Armand thought he was made of Teflon, untouchable. He made the mistake of trusting his partners in crime.

Unbeknownst to his enemies, Armand had a safety net. His spies were in every boardroom and office in the company. He had his own plans to become very, very, very rich in the process. But he needed help.

This was where Big Pete, Tiny Murdoch, and Maurice "The Leech" Lévesque came into the picture.

When they were kids Maurice, and Armand attended school together in a small village in France.

A fact scrubbed from company records, because if the company found out he was once associated with a notorious jewel thief he would never get away with what they were about to attempt.

Safety nets were important.

Maurice had never been caught — or even under suspicion by the authorities — for his illegal activities. Consequently, he could travel with complete anonymity anywhere in the world. Big Pete and Tiny were the worker bees of this operation.

They did all the heavy lifting and were well compensated for their part of the many successful robberies planned and executed by Maurice and his team.

The expert thief's policy was to steal from the rich who kept their valuables off the books. Insurance agents and the police wouldn't be looking for the perpetrators of the crimes. They didn't even have any idea where to begin looking if they pulled off each heist as planned.

It was a convenient and lucrative operation for all involved.

Of course, this didn't guarantee there weren't people looking for them. Many of these rich people were upset about losing their valuable trinkets. They would send private contractors to investigate.

So far, no one had gotten close to the truth.

The truth was the rich victims often bought back their own merchandise at the next high priced auction even though the pieces looked very different from how they had last seen them.

Ironic, eh what? thought Pete with amusement.

He stood next to the cowed guard riding upward to the top floor in the high-speed elevator. When the guard checked with Armand's office the Vice President's personal assistant growled at him to stop delaying Mr. Rustica.

The elevator car was rife with the scent of the guard's cologne. It reminded Pete of rose water.

Kinda girly for a big guy like him. But what the hell. I'm not his mother.

The office over looked the city through a wall of glass spread out like a shining monument to man's ingenuity. The view took Pete's breath away. He had never been this high over the city.

Armand sat behind his glass desk. Tiny and Maurice sat in shiny red leather wing chairs in front of Armand's desk. Armand looked so regal in his five thousand dollar custom made suit. His black hair was streaked with traces of gray.

His weathered face broke into a smile as Peter entered the room followed by Armand's assailant, a comely redhead dressed in a beige pantsuit who smelled of green apples.

"Thank you, Miss Taylor, please get a chair for Mr. Rustica —"

"Call me Pete, please," said Pete to Armand as Miss Taylor lifted and carried, with one hand, another of the red leather chairs away from where it sat against a wall then set it down next to Tiny's chair.

Impressive. Pete admired the woman's upper body strength. She probably doubled as Armand's bodyguard. Having a bodyguard that's easy on the eyes is a rich man's bonus.

Soon I'll be able to afford five who look like her.

Tiny's amused gaze followed Miss Taylor's rear end as she turned and left the room closing the door to the outer office behind her.

"My, my," breathed Tiny.

"Knock it off, Tiny," said Pete jokingly. "Ya'll soon be fightin' broads like her off with yore big stick."

Tiny snorted. "I'll show her a big stick awright —" To punctuate his point he grabbed his crotch.

"Will you two please cease the juvenile banter. We have serious work ahead," said Maurice dryly.

Pete and Tiny looked at each other and shrugged.

I hate it when he talks all high and mighty in fronta clients.

Some guys would think he was puttin' 'em down for not bein' so educated. Of course, Maurice and us we been makin' a lotta dough together over the years so he must be jokin'. If there's one thing I'm good at it's readin' people."

"You bring the item?" said Armand, his tone anxious.

Pete wanted to laugh aloud, but he managed to contain himself. "Yeah. I have the item."

Guy musta seen one too many movies. Dork.

Pete slapped the hard-shelled black leather briefcase on the desk. He thumbed the catches on the left and right of the handle and they popped loudly with a metal-on-metal snap in the silence of the office.

Pete picked the data chip from a pouch designed to store and protect it then handed it to Maurice. A small plastic disk — about the size of a large washer — contained five trillion megabytes of data within its memory.

"Is this the one we need? As we discussed?" asked Armand.

Pete was getting seriously irritated by the guy, but he nodded any way forcing a placid expression to his face.

Maurice must have detected Pete's annoyance because he said, "As we agreed this simulation will allow us to practice the robbery countless times until we have it perfected —"

"How long will it take — I don't have a lot of time you know —"

Maurice held up one hand to silence his old school chum. Armand went quiet his eyes flitting back and forth over the three men sitting across from him.

Maurice cleared his throat then said, "We need the big lab on the seventh floor. It will take ten days to practice, then two to affect the robbery. The cops will buzz like angry hornets for several weeks afterward, but I'm not concerned with them. By the time they piece together what happened we'll be in a neutral country, safe from prosecution."

"Are there any neutral countries anymore?" said Armand.

A crooked smile crossed Maurice's face and his dark eyes flashed with humor. His fine boned hands smoothed his slate-gray dress slacks and he rolled his shoulders slightly beneath his gray tweed sport coat.

"But of course, my old friend. I know all the right people in all the low places."

Armand eased back in his executive chair and laughed.

Pete stole a glance at Tiny. They both shrugged seemingly uncomprehending. What the heck were the two men were talking about? They were off the books. They weren't going anywhere as far as Pete was concerned.

***

Pete materialized within the walls of the vault. He stood frozen in place for a moment until the containment beam dissipated. Good thing too. If the quantum computer didn't reassemble your molecules in just the right place it was goodbye world and hello oblivion.

He looked around amazed at what he was seeing. It all looked so real. The vault even smelled of money. How freakin' real do these things get.

He'd always thought the PRIE's were designed for high-end gamers. Those types didn't need to steal. They just played at crime. It wasn't very long ago when people thought a video game could make someone commit a crime. Morons. The idea was just plain stupid.

Of course, the PRIE was much more than those old passive game systems.

The gamer actually was able to interact with characters and change the outcome of the game. Safety systems were designed so the user wouldn't be hurt, but gamers could be shot, stabbed, or blown to bits, or make love to the woman of their dreams. It seemed as real to the gamer as the real world.

"Talk about your safe sex," Pete mused.

What you couldn't use the system for was to commit a crime. Even a simulated crime like the one they were attempting. A black lab — one that would create anything for anyone for a price — created the program they were using to test the robbery. The lone downside was the safety protocols had to be taken out. Even holo-bullets can kill.

Oh well. Who wants to live forever?

Real people didn't have a use for such expensive toys. Million-billionaires bought these things. While there were plenty of them around Pete and Tiny certainly weren't in that category. The most they'd ever made in one year of working for Maurice was a hundred grand. Certainly not enough to buy an SUV never mind one of these expensive gadgets.

Armand's money paid for the black lab version and Pete knew it had taken most of his available cash. No wonder the guy was desperate. It was all or nothing. A real crapshoot. As it was for them.

They had never been on the cops radar given the attention this job was going to draw it would have to be their last. In the real vault, the hidden monitors couldn't be bypassed so their images would be flashed around the world when the robbery was discovered. They would just have to ensure they left the country ahead of the cops. Simple.

Yeah, right.

Of course, they planned to use the toy for far more than its designers originally intended.

They ran the robbery simulation seventeen times without one successful test.

The plan involved using a teleporter to materialize inside the vault containing the patents for every known piece of new tech that was acquired during contact with the Vetsa.

The Vetsa was an alien race that willingly shared their technology with Earth's industrialists. What the aliens didn't bargain on was the ruthlessness of Earth's most ambitious men and women.

The super rich wiped out all life on the aliens home world using their own technology and weapons. Not humanities finest hour.

A consortium of industrialists quickly applied for patents for the alien tech.

Humans now had access to teleporters, flying cars, guns that were encoded to one person's brain chemistry, and this holo-technology. The Personal Recreation Interface Entertainment (or PRIE) system made it possible to simulate any environment programmed by the user. Science fiction was now science reality.

Pete released the strap that held his .45 in place and held it up as the door to the outer vault area slide rapidly open and two guards rushed in wearing body armor. Pete methodically killed them both with one shot each in the center of their forehead. They dropped like two sacks of potatoes with hard thumps onto the tiled floor. Their drawn pistols skittered across the ties to stop at Pete's feet.

The iron scent of blood penetrated the air masking the smell of the money.

During the first two simulations, the two sim-guards had surprised him grazing his left shoulder in the resulting shoot out. He failed to notice they were wearing protective vests and had shot them each in the chest.

This slowed them but they kept coming and it had taken him several seconds to realize his mistake and take them down. Pain and the sight of your own blood were good teachers. He had to agree with Maurice.

He was lucky.

Pete stepped over the two pistols just as Tiny materialized. He was wearing the body pack with the C4. Working quickly the two men squeezed the C4 from its packaging onto the center two titanium lined safety deposit boxes. The stuff looked like plumbers putty, but with more of a kick.

The boxes were eighteen inches by eighteen inches square. The patent certificates were secured inside. Pete licked his dry lips as they finished then he stuck in the detonators and set the timers for ten seconds.

He nodded to Tiny and they pressed their recall buttons simultaneously. The two thieves dematerialized and were standing on the lab floor looking at the large monitor affixed to one wall.

Within seconds, the screen became distorted, and as was the case seventeen times before, the floor beneath their feet trembled from the force of the blast. The screen settled down once more. Gray smoke obscured their view until powerful air exchange fans designed to remove smoke in case of fire sucked the smoke from the vault room.

Tiny glanced at Pete and smiled knowingly.

The two thieves pressed the buttons on their belts again and in the blink of an eye stood in the hazy air of the vault were looking at two safety despots boxes split open like fresh cantaloupe.

Instinctively Tiny reached inside the box nearest him. He froze and his face visibly paled. He stumbled backward holding his damaged hand. The boxes were booby-trapped.

Tiny groaned and blood dripped onto the floor from his nearly severed hand. There was a large gash across the back of his hand cutting through the skin exposing the bone in his wrist.

This wasn't good. If Tiny's blood was found inside the real vault his DNA would lead the cops right to him. Could Tiny stand up to interrogation? Or would he talk to save his own skin?

Pete wasn't certain. Nope this 'isn't good.

"Hold." Pete and Tiny materialized back in the lab facing a distraught Armand and a very worried looking Maurice. Peter had never seen his boss look so worried.

"You okay, boss?" asked Pete. Stupid question, Peter. Moron.

"Very funny, Pete —" Tiny hit the floor hard and lay still. He'd lost a lot of blood and had no doubt fainted.

"What about him?" asked Pete, gazing at his friend laying unconscious on the floor curled in the fetal position.

"Take him to the infirmary on the first floor," said Armand curtly.

Pete shrugged and bent down to gather Tiny in his massive arms. He cradled him like a baby and then headed for the elevators.

***

"Test Nineteen," Pete said into the mike.

Within microseconds the massive computing power of the quantum computer than ran PRIE, the teleporter simultaneously set up the simulation, and he dematerialized.

As before, once in the vault he shot the two guards as if he was shooting at aluminum ducks at the carnival then set the charges and the timers.

Once the smoke from the explosion cleared, Pete stood staring at the two boxes. One contained a deadly trap that killed his friend — unbeknownst to them the blades in the trap were tipped with puffer fish venom — Tiny hadn't fainted he'd died. The other contained the certificates that were worth limitless wealth. They would be kings of all they surveyed.

For the first time in his life the question Pete faced was is this worth it?

Closing his eyes, he ignored the box Tiny had put his hand in and instead reached inside the other one.

Nothing happened until his fingers brushed over paper. Hen snapped back his hand. His eyes flew open and frantically inspected his appendage for damage. With a deep sense of relief, he let out the breath he'd been holding and felt the urge to laugh.

Finally.

He quickly reached inside and pulled out the sim-certificates then slapped the button on his belt with the flat of his hand. Nothing happened so this time he gingerly pressed the button again.

Again, nothing.

What the — ?

An alarm began to wail and a wall of steel bars appeared from the ceiling blocking his exit via the door the two dead guards had come through.

Something was seriously wrong.

"Ah, Mr. Rustica I presume," said a deep baritone voice on the opposite side of the bars.

Pete walked toward the man his pistol drawn held waist level in front of him. Standing with an arrogant smirk on his lips on the other side of the bars was a man of medium height and weight wearing the uniform of the secret police.

In his youth, Pete had been a member of that organization so he knew the attire well. He also recognized the insignia on the collar. The man with the brown nearly trimmed beard, shot through with gray streaks, was a colonel.

"I hate officers," Pete murmured.

"I seem to have the drop on you, colonel," said Pete waving the pistol to emphasize his point.

The colonel chuckled and crossed his arms over his chest. "Yes. I believe you do at that, Mr. Rustica —"

"Call me Pete."

"And you can call me Colonel Driver, Pete."

Pete feigned surprise. "Why so formal, Driver?"

Colonel Driver frowned. "Well you see, Pete, you and I are going to be spending a lot of time together."

It was Pete's turn to laugh. "I don't think so, Colonel. As you can see I have the gun."

Out of the corner of one eye, Pete saw a blur of movement coming from behind him. He attempted to turn but was too late. He felt a hard, painful snap against the back of his head and he fell on his side to the floor. His world exploded in a dizzying array of lights and spots that danced across his vision.

Dazed but still conscious he looked up at the Colonel who was now standing over him the bars having retreated into the ceiling.

"I don't understand," gasped Pete weakly. He detected the scent of the waxy polish coming from Drivers gleaming, calf-height boots.

"You're a deserter. You were convicted *in abstentia* by a military court. You will be taken into custody and serve your life sentence in Leavenworth."

"I have rights —"

"Deserters have no rights."

"But I committed the perfect crime."

"Mr. Rustica, there is no such thing as the perfect crime." Driver's eyes flashed. "Especially when a grief stricken woman is involved."

Pete's eyes looked puzzled.

Driver smiled mirthlessly. "Miss Taylor is one of our agents. She tipped us off what you and the others were doing. We're not interested in prosecution of the thievery, but I think you'll find your partners in crime will all be resting comfortably as wards of the state for quite some time."

Pete felt two sets of strong hands grab his arms and left him from the floor. His feet dragged so the two cops each held him up by placing one of his arms over their shoulders. They each had one around his waist to support his weight.

Driver was about to walk away when he paused and appeared thoughtful.

"And one more thing," he said slowly. "We would never have found out about you without Tiny Murdoch's death. I'm truly sorry about him, but as the French say, 'Ce la vie.'

"Of course, the real loser in this little drama is Miss Taylor. She truly loved Tiny."

The Eliminators

"IMPOSSIBLE..." I BREATHED.

The rapid beating of my heart eclipsed the incessant growl of big city traffic coming from the street below the office window.

It — the spectral figure — levitated a meter above the scored and heavily traveled hardwood floor of our cramped, dusty office.

We're located in a two-story walk up, near the corner of Main and Hastings Streets on the east side of Vancouver. Harry and I have operated our PI business from the 50-year-old-plus office building for the past five years. I sometimes forget five years has passed since we'd opened The Eliminators Paranormal Investigative Service together as partners. Most people called us The Eliminators for short. (I certainly prefer this over the unflattering E-PIS our detractors call us.)

The truth was we were secretly under contract to the City of Vancouver's finest. Not that the VPD chief would ever admit we often worked for the cops when they were faced with unexplained paranormal crime. The chief's office was just two blocks from where I stood yet he had never even set foot inside our door.

His kiss-ass assistant, Blake "Blakey" Thomas acted as his intermediary. Blakey is such a weasel.

The press dubs us the Ghostbusters named I suppose after that Dan Ackroyd movie in the eighties. In reality, we had never seen an actual ghost until this moment. And the one standing before me looked very much like my mother.

I shivered in the cold air. Unusual for an August afternoon when the outside temperature neared forty degrees Celsius, and normally even warmer in here.

The woman-shaped phantom stood, or should I say floated, on the opposite side of my scarred forties era pine desk indeed looked the spitting image of my mother. Expect for the dark pupiless eyes she could easily pass as Mom's doppelganger. A twin maybe. A dead twin perhaps, but still a mirror image of my mother.

Not that I knew if dear old Mom was alive, or dead. I hadn't seen her in a long time.

Dressed in tan walking shorts, a mustard yellow sleeveless tee shirt, and brown leather sandals Mom's gaze was unflinchingly fixed on me. Her ensemble must be all the rage amongst the best-dressed ghosts these days.

"Huh…what…what…do you want…" I managed to stammer from between frozen lips. The sweetened coffee I had been sipping turned sour in my mouth.

Out of the corner of one eye I saw my partner Harry — only the scuffed soles of his brown leather shoes were visible — his tree trunk like legs were crossed atop his equally ancient desk. His muscular fingers were laced across his wide chest and his cool blue eyes were fixated on the ghost. That was Harry. Cool as the proverbial cucumber.

He had been in the process of writing up the invoice for our latest client when the ghost suddenly appeared.

Mr. Wallace hired us to follow his wife, who he thought was unfaithful. For this one we didn't even have to leave the office. Easy money.

Harry's gift for foretelling the future meant he had seen Mrs. Wallace's lover's death in a seven-car pile up on Route One.

It was going to rain hard the next day and Harry saw the guy's green Dodge Ram roll over and burst into flames. The guy was barbecue.

An ugly scene true, but it meant some much funds would join their meager cousins in the bank.

Poor Harry. He didn't much care for his so-called "gift" in cases like the guy with the truck. I had to agree seeing and feeling the guys terror as he burned to death was not much of gift.

Though he is able to see future events he is unable to change them in any way. If he saw the country was about to be nuked he would be helpless to stop it. Sure, he could warn people, and leave the country himself, but the nukes would still fall. Talk about the ultimate raw deal.

Me? I can move stuff with my mind. I always figured that's why Mom left us, and Dad drank himself to death. They just couldn't handle my gift.

In the Wallace's case, Mrs. Wallace would not be cheating with that guy again. And she wouldn't cheat with anyone else. Harry had seen that as well.

I offered my opinion that Mrs. Wallace must have really loved the guy — the lover, not the husband — Harry wasn't so sure.

He thought Mrs. Wallace was damned scared of what might happen to her.

She suspected her husband was behind the accident. Kinda like that Harrison Ford movie, about a lawyer whose wife murders his mistress. Being in the PI business means you encounter a lot of loonies.

For five years we had been at this location, and for five years we have been trying, without success, to move The Eliminators Paranormal Investigative Service up the PI food chain. We were eager to get closer to the really big bucks downtown. Simple really. If only we could snag one of those upscale clients — and if the press stopped calling us a couple of nuts — then we might stand a real chance at success.

The slumlord that ran this two-story walk-up demanded more rent every year. This meant we had less and less for the luxuries, like food.

"You can't be my mother," I said to the silent apparition. "I haven't seen her in fifteen years. Nor do I want to. Ever."

To emphasize my point I used my telekinesis to fly a white china coffee cup off the makeshift shelf I had installed over the drip coffee pot directly at its head. It passed through her then shattered with a loud bang against the opposite wall, near the sagging gray metal file cabinet.

Harry sighed. "Do ya really have to do that?"
"Sorry. I — "

"You have to kill me," said the ghost suddenly. Her voice was soft and echoed as if she were speaking from inside a steel drum.

Harry suddenly fell backward to land with a loud bang against the cheap tile floor. "Oh. My. God," he said.

A shiver ran through me. Harry knew something. His gift was telling him something-- something bad. His face was pale; as pale as the white dress shirt he wore under his smoke-gray suit jacket. I hated his ties, but never said so to his face anyway. This one was a ghastly flora pattern

Do something, numb nuts, I said to myself. But it was as if I were frozen where I stood. Fear gripped me and my limbs refused to respond to my brains instructions.

I detected a faint odor of ozone in the air. It was as if an electrical charge surrounded the ghost of my mother. This is too weird.

"My son was always useless," she said.

I didn't have to listen to this crap. Before I could stop myself years of pent up frustration and anger spilled out of me. "You ran out on us, Dad was devastated — I was only twelve."

"All true. But you don't know the whole truth." The ghost of Mary Alice O'Shay turned to face me.

"Your father beat me, or had your forgotten about that part of our happy home life."

I felt my ears grow warm. "No. But Dad had—issues."

"Dad was a drunk." She snorted in disgust.

Now as I said, Harry and I had never seen a real ghost before. We had certainly uncovered a few frauds, but this spirit didn't look like faked special effects. Not, like the case Harry and I solved when the disgraced special effects guy used SFX to scare a widow out of her family fortune.

He'd blackmailed her by haunting her with her deceased husbands ghost. The "ghost" said she had murdered him for his money. All true of course, she had certainly murdered her husband ten years before. But, the special effects guy just could not resist the urge to use his talents to fool the old lady. Scared her to death. Heart attack.

We caught the special effects guy the old-fashioned way. Too bad really. At the time, I thought it would be nice to see the ghost of her dead husband. Now I wasn't so certain.

"Huh, Jimmy..."said Harry. "I don't wanta interrupt your family reunion, but it seems to me we have a larger issue here. Like why is a ghost standing in our office?"

Mary chuckled. "Of course. Harry's right. James, you and I will have to work through this baggage of ours later. Besides, there isn't a lot of time."

"For what?" I said. My eyes narrowed, while my voice echoed my suspicion.

"Like I started to say, before we began our trip down memory lane, you have to kill me. Within the next hour," she said. The way she said the words, they seemed so matter-of-fact, it sent a chill through me.

If she needed to die then that was one thing. The far greater problem was how do you kill someone who is already dead?

***

Over the years, Harry and I have seen a lot of strange things. If people knew there were vampires, werewolves, monsters of every shape and kind, and aliens from planets too distant to be seen by Hubble, walking among them they would freak. But the ghost of my dead mother? That definitely ranked highest on my strange scale.

And, it got even stranger when Mary explained she was the ghost of her future self. Twenty years in the future to be exact. She apparently died after being in a coma for twenty years. A coma caused by being hit by a car, today.

Somehow, I would kill her so she wouldn't have to spend the next twenty years in a coma before she succumbed.

My head hurt. "Nope. I don't think so, Mom. Besides, why should I help you? I don't even like you!"

Mary hung her head. "Tell him, Harry."

Harry dropped his shoes to the floor with thump. The odor of disturbed dust permeated the air. "She's right Jimmy. She will be hit by the car today and be in the coma for twenty years…"

I felt Mary's dark eyes gazing at me. "Son. James. I am still your mother. I love you. I know I haven't been there for you for a long time." Her voice was gentle, enveloping me with its soft summer breeze quality.

"You bet your ass," I said. Even as I said the words, I knew I was being too harsh. What galled me most was she was right.

When I first met Harry in grade ten, at John Oliver Secondary, he told me my whole life story in ten minutes. It was as if the guy worked for Sixty Minutes. Now here was my mother's damn ghost confirming my best friend's twisted tale. Harry warned me would be days like this. And Harry is never wrong.

"I'm so sorry, James. Sorry I wasn't there. Sorry I…" She paused. "I'm going to be hit by a car today."

"Then I'll be in a coma for the next twenty years before I die. The police will track you down as my only living relative, and you're going to tell them not to pull the plug on me. You're so consumed with guilt that you just can't let me go. I don't want you to go through that, son."

I glared at Harry whose face was a shade of pink. He had never told me this about my mother. What good was a guy who left out the most important parts about a guy's mother? The messy bits I call them.

He shrugged his broad shoulders. "Hey. Don't look at me. Sure I saw her accident, and the coma thingy, but I thought you didn't wanta see her. I mean you always say..."

"Never mind." I cut him off. "We'll talk about this later."

Mary's ghost floated to the window over looking the late morning traffic. Cars honked their horns and trucks rumbled by below our window. The odor of burnt gasoline wafted in from the street. She gazed into the street with a longing I had had never seen in a living person, never mind a dead one.

Her voice became small. "I don't want to live the next twenty years of my earthly existence in a useless husk." She whirled to face me her expression grim.

"You have to kill me."

What could I do? Harry said the car would hit her, and she is — or rather was — oh shit — my head was spinning. I nodded. "Yeah, I guess so."

"Whoa," Hal said holding his hands up as if he were surrendering to Castro's army. "You might be charged with murder. You can't just go around killing people ya know. Besides we don't know where Mary is right now."

I shot him a warning look. "Don't you start with me." I knew perfectly well that if I were going to be caught Harry would know already. And somehow I knew that he knew I wouldn't be caught. (This stuff is just too weird for words.) He'd already seen it. Good thing neither of us have criminal minds or he and I would make a killing on horseracing or at the casinos. Honesty really does have its drawbacks.

Mary's ghost pointed out the window to the busy street. I moved to look where Mary was pointing. Sure enough, there walking down the cracked sidewalk, was the very much alive Mary O'Shay, the former Mrs. Ivan Rusinski.

Harry and I looked at each other. He wore a stunned expressions on his faces which I'm sure mirrored my own. My mother had been this close to me and I had never even realized it.

I stood straight and looked at my partner. "So, Harry, how do I kill her?"

***

Mary's ghost told me she was only visible to Harry and I. And that she could have be visible to anyone she wanted to see her. She didn't want anyone else to see her but us at the moment. Strange how the rules of the paranormal so often turn out to be so simple.

Even more strange was that in some sort of cosmic joke if we succeeded then a woman would be murdered — this was really, really crazy.

We rode in silence in my '82 Buick. Mary sat — if that's what ghosts do — in the back seat gazing around at the city that flashed by.

"I remember how this looked." An occasional glance in the rear view told me she was taking everything in with her strange eye as we neared the suburb of New Westminster. The sparkling neon signs of the movie and entertainment complex known as Metropolis were behind us.

Mary's eyes were as wide as a child's as we passed the massive entertainment complex. "I don't remember this," she said in a tiny voice

Our destination beyond New West is Surrey.

It was nearly noon and the sun had warmed the inside of the ancient Buick. The faux leather seats stuck to my pants. I wasn't sure if it was the heat, or my nerves, making me sweat so profusely.

We arrive to find the sky train parking lot is packed with cars. Not unusual at this time of day since the lot is for downtown commuters who save money by parking their cars here then ride the rapid transit service to the downtown business district.

The parking lots were well known to cops and crooks alike as the car thief strip mall. Every make and model of car and truck imaginable was lined up in neat rows ready for inspection by their new "owners".

When we arrived, we saw the bike patrol cop in her lemon yellow vest, with the word 'POLICE' in bold black lettering on the back, pedaling away on her taxpayer funded thousand dollar mountain bike. Perfect timing.

She didn't give us a second glance as she went by. Two guys in suits — regardless if the suits looked like their owners had slept in them — certainly weren't your usual car thief type. In normal circumstances she'd be right. Then these were far from normal circumstances.

We drove slowly through the parking lot until we found an older model Toyota with button locks. It would be the easiest to steal.

I stepped out and used my telekinesis to unlock the driver's door. As I did so, Harry slid behind the wheel of the Buick.

Harry his pale forehead beaded with sweat motioned for me to hurry. His bloodless knuckles gripped the steering wheel. I had never seen him like this. His body trembled with nerves as he kneaded the plastic wheel as if he were making bread dough. My normally cool partner was scared. To tell the truth so was I.

The door squealed metal-on-metal as I opened it. Harry squeezed his eyes tight. Damn!

I quickly sat behind the wheel and went to work on the steering column. I had stolen a couple of cars in my impetuous youth so I certainly knew how.

The plastic cover over the steering column came off easily and I managed to find the wires. I cut them with the box cutter I brought with me. I striped the wires and crossed them correctly. I twisted the yellow and blue wires together then brought the green and white wires together to create the spark to kick over the starter motor.

Nothing. No spark.

Beads of sweat formed on my brow, and dripped into my eyes, blinding me. I tried again. Nothing.

I slammed the dashboard hard in frustration with my fist. Deciding I had wasted too much time I stepped out then realized the dashboard didn't look right. Someone had installed an after factory immobilizer.

I shook my head and silently chastised myself.

"What's the matter," said Harry, his voice an urgent whisper.

"Immobilizer. We have to find another car."

We started to cruise the lot again and quickly found an even older car. It was pale green '72 Impala. Harry knew it because he'd owned one just like it in the late seventies.

A pig on gas, but it would more than do the job. The big V8 and the heavy steel body made it the perfect weapon.

***

Once back downtown, Mary directed us to the street she would be on this time of day. It was in Gastown, a tourist area of restored brick buildings and cobblestone streets named after Gassy Jack, a nineteenth century bar owner and local rascal.

In the center of the area was an old steam clock. The cobblestones made for a bumpy ride, but the tourists thought the streets were quaint. To me it was just a jarring joyless ride for the spine.

As we bumped over the worn cobblestones my teeth rattled. Just great.

Harry parked the old Buick, now officially dubbed the "getaway car", on a side street while I would drive the Impala to the spot where Mary was going to be (at least according to our time traveling ghost).

I would use the heavy car run her down and kill her. I was to make sure she was dead by backing up and running over her again.

We knew we'd be changing history, at least Mary's personal history. Of course, the history of the man who'd originally run her down would also be altered, in his case for the better.

What we knew for sure is a car would strike Mary; nothing could change that one fact. It might not be today, but it would happen. And, she'd be in a coma if I didn't help her. To avoid countless years of silent suffering she would die today by my hand.

I shook my head. I now knew what it felt to be Harry and I hated the pain in my belly. But I knew what I had to do. She'd begged me. And even after years of estrangement she was still my mother.

Our plan meant I would abandon the Impala in an alley and escape in the Buick. Hopefully we would get away before anyone would identify us.

"Gotta do it fast," Mary said. "Like Al Pacino in the first Godfather movie when he shoots the gangster and the dirty cop."

Harry and I had forgone the usual PI baggy suits and ties, instead preferring to don jeans and tee shirts. In addition I had added a New York Yankees ball cap and mirrored sunglasses. Harry, the Mr. GQ of our little firm, hated the disguises, but it would lessen the chances of being identified.

As I sat in the Impala I felt my stomach churn. A trace of bile invaded my mouth when I spotted the very much alive Mary O'Shay coming down the sidewalk toward me.

She looked happy. Doubt nearly forced me from the car to warn her about the other guy. But a greater fear of my own failure kept me glued to the seat. Harry said the accident was going to happen no matter what I did.

Mary would either die or be in a coma. What kind of choices were these? Why couldn't I just hit the guy who would hit her, and save her from the coma?

Harry said the only thing we could change was the time of Mary's accident, not the inevitability of it. Harry is always right.

My hands worried the steering wheel until I thought the pale green plastic would come off on my hands.

The vision of her struck by the car became suddenly very clear in my mind. The scream. The blood. The sickening smack of her lifeless body hitting the pavement. I closed my eyes and struggled to push the sight and sounds of what was about to happen from my mind. And there was something else…

My eyes popped open as the passenger door flew open. It was Harry. "I'm with you, buddy."

"I know," I said. "Let's go."

The Impala moved easily into traffic. As I neared the crosswalk, I picked up speed. The cobblestones made the car bounce into the air as if it wanted to leave the ground.

The powerful engine roared and the wind rushed in through the open windows as we hurled toward my mother. There she was frozen at the sight of the roaring pride of General Motors racing full speed toward her.

I closed my eyes and hit the accelerator hard. Harry screamed. I heard the slap of flesh landing hard as it pounded over the windshield of the car followed by the screams of people on the street around us.

It happened so quickly I thought for a second I might have missed her, until I opened my eyes to glance in the rearview mirror. My heart leapt into my throat.

Framed by the mirror, in the middle of the street behind us, lay a crumpled human form. With both feet I slammed the brake pedal hard causing us to be thrown violently forward. The air filled with the smell of burnt rubber and the screeched of tires as we came to a stop. The seat belt holding me pressed against me until it hurt my chest.

I hit the shift lever into reverse then stepped hard on the accelerator. The car raced backward over the prone lump lying in the middle of the street. It felt like we had hit a speed bump.

I stopped again, shifted into drive, then drove over the body for the last time and headed away. Out of the corner of one eye, I saw the shocked looks of the people watching the horrific spectacle.

Oh, my God. What have I done!

I steered the heavy car around a corner and then into a deserted alley. I felt as if I were moving in thick air as we climbed out of the car leaving the doors open and ran headlong down the dank, dirty alley. The sour smell of garbage, coming from the rusted steel dumpsters that lined the alley, assaulted my senses as we ran. Hot tears streamed down my cheeks.

I killed my own mother!

After what seemed like an eternity, we made it to the Buick, and I threw my sunglasses to the street. Once inside Harry started, the car and we sped away.

He quickly reduced speed as cop cars and an ambulance screamed passed us, going in the opposite direction.

I glanced at Harry, tears blurring eyes that brimmed over with regret and grief. He shook his head sadly and I knew she was dead. I have not seen her for fifteen years and now she was dead.

I heard a soft voice behind me say, "It's okay, son. I know you love me."

***

The headline in the paper the next day stated a stolen car had killed an unidentified pedestrian in a cross walk in Gastown. It was labeled a hit-and-run by the cops, probably — or so the reporter presumed, by kids' joy riding. The cops said they would catch the culprits very soon. The article ended by saying the victims name would not be released until the next of kin were contacted. Of course I already knew the name.

Rain pelted the windows and the smell of fresh coffee permeated the tiny office. Harry's dark eyes, his long legs crossed rested on his desk, were the saddest I had ever seen them. I felt numb.

"I guess Blakey's gonna be calling," murmured Harry.

"Yeah. I guess so."

"What we gonna tell him?"

I shrugged my shoulders. I had no idea. "If he asks we'll tell him we were at a funeral."

"Yeah…" There was nothing else to say.

For several minutes the only sounds in our office came from the incessant ticking of the plastic battery operated clock that hung off the wall. Finally, Harry said, "Where's the ghost?"

I sighed then lifted my coffee mug with the Disney characters dancing happily across it to my lips. "She said she had to do something. But that she'd be here."

The room grew cold. "Hi, boys," said a cheery voice. Too cheery for a dead person in my reckoning.

"What the hell are you so happy about?" I said my voice as bitter as the overcooked coffee.

Mary chuckled. "I'm staying. I have permission."

I moved my legs off my desk and sat forward in my chair my hands gripping the arms of my chair. "What the hell are you talking about?" I said.

"I'm your new partner. I'm going to work cases with you boys." Harry shook his head and snorted.

I thought about asking her who gave her permission, then decided against it. I didn't want to know.

This turn of events pretty much confirmed it: we are officially the strangest PI firm on the planet.

Children of the Monster

I stood shivering in front of the massive oak door staring with fascination at the devils head doorknocker the size of a small terrier. The ornate iron ornament was at eye level in the center of the scarred wood. My mentor, friend and, like I, professional Pinkerton's agent, Noel Stoker stood next to me on the stone stoop.

I must have been out of my mind when I agreed to accompany Noel to a cold, dank and smelly village named Limberburger. The Baron Frankenstein sent us a letter requesting we come to his castle?

Noel must have thought I'm a fool to believe such nonsense.

I'd rather hoped Limberburger was a pub in Soho. I buried my ice-cold hands in the pockets of my coat.

Jokes on me. Ha, ha...

Noel must have known of the cold mists that swirl through this valley in early winter. He was wearing his father's thick wool topcoat and heavy gloves. His balding head was covered with his favorite grey felt fedora. I on the other hand wore my thinner fall trench coat. I was dressed for London drizzle not Limberburger winter.

Noel glanced at me his hazel eyes impatient then grasped the heavy knocker and pounded it against the door once, then twice more in rapid succession. Thunderous thumps greeted our ears as the sound of metal on wood echoed from the other side of the massive door. Then a voice thick and gruff and edged with sleep called out from behind the door.

"I'm coming for goodness sake! What's your hurry! How'm I supposed to get my beauty sleep?"

The mist swirled about my ankles like spider webs as we waited.

After several seconds I heard the sounds of numerous locks being sprung and latches being let loose. I took one step back as the door finally swung inward. Its steel hinges squealed due to centuries of rust.

The man — well not a man exactly, for his face, was misshapen as if it were made of clay had one eye socket set lower than the other.

The nose, which was as crooked as a mountain trail, was narrow with a bump in the middle. His skin was pale almost translucent and his eyes were of two different colors, one brown and one green — greeted us with a grunt and a look of distain.

In a right hand larger than is normal for a man of his diminutive stature he held a silver candleholder with three receptacles. The three candles in the receptacles were lit and the golden flames cast long shadows across the darkened entrance. I could feel the heat that emanated from the candles from where I stood on the stone stoop. He smells of cheese. And he's a hunchback.

"Yes! What do you want?"

Noel, ever the gentleman of regal propriety, bowed slightly at the waist and tipped his hat. "We are seeking an audience with the Baron Frankenstein. We have come some distance at his request." Noel reached into the inside pocket of his suit jacket within the folds of the great coat and withdrew the letter we received a fortnight ago at our offices in London.

The Baron had written us seeking our assistance in locating a valuable *object'á art*. At least that's what Noel told our boss, Mr. Thomas. I didn't believe him but Mr. Thomas seemed pleased to get rid of us. At least that's what his grunt seemed to convey.

With a twist of the tip of his waxed mustache Noel handed the letter to the gnarled dwarf.

"My name is Noel Stoker, and this is my colleague Denis Doyle. We represent the Pinkerton Detective Agency."

The hunchback eyed the letter skeptically then sighed heavily and stepped back. "Come in."

Noel shot me a wink then stepped through the doorway. Once inside the hunchback closed the heavy door and I watched enthralled as he re-engaged all of the numerous locks.

They're certainly security conscious around here.

He must have seen my interest in this activity. "You can never be too careful. There are children of the night who would roam this valley. Sometimes they come home very late."

The interior was cloaked in inky darkness but in the dim light I could make out the wide spiral staircase made of mahogany that disappeared upward into the gloom.

I shivered again. Not from fear but due to the draft of cold air that washed over us. The evil looking dwarf didn't seem to notice the cold though he was dressed in only a nightshirt, and sleeping cap.

I looked at his feet and was surprised to see he was wearing large fuzzy bunny slippers.

How odd.

"My master will be down shortly."

"How does he know we're here?" I blurted.

The hunchback's twisted features became a smile I would not want to see twice in my life time. The creature's yellow crooked teeth and grotesque mouth would have repulsed even father's famed fictional detective.

Noel nodded. "Thank you, Igor."

The dwarf frowned. "Name's Herman. Igor was my father."

Noel grinned and twisted his moustache as his dark eyes scanned the dimly lit surroundings. "Yes, of course."

Herman the hunchback grunted and walked to a side table where there was another of the three candle stick holders and used the one he carried to light the candles. He then turned and shuffled to the spiral staircase. It was then I noticed his left leg was withered and he had to drag it behind him.

No wonder it took him so long to come to the door. Noel must have had the same thought because he eyed me knowingly and nodded toward Herman who had started to climb the stairs.

"Good night...Ig...I mean, Herman."

Herman stopped and looked back over his shoulder at a grinning Noel. "The master will be down shortly." He soon disappeared into a door at the top of the stairs.

I fidgeted as the sound of a wolf howl was carried with the cold draft. "Spooky place uh, Noel?"

Noel smiled. "Yes. Quite."

"Do you think the Baron Frankenstein is —"

"— The model for Mary Shelly's monster?" One eyebrow arched up Noel's forehead and there was a twinkle in his eye. I nodded as I pulled the flaps around the collar of my trench coat tighter around my neck.

Noel shrugged. "Probably. I know my father seemed to think so." His eyes narrowed. "Of course my father used a fifteenth century Transylvanian Prince as his model for his book, so I'm not surprised that Shelly would use a Limberburger Baron. There are numerous legends surrounding this castle."

"Yes there are, Mr. Stoker."

I looked around for the source of the voice and realized it came from the top of the staircase. In the darkness I could make out a human figure.

"Baron Frankenstein, I presume?" Noel moved to the half moon shaped side table and picked up the candleholder.

He carried it the bottom of the stairs and squinted into the darkness as the meager light from the candles made the shadows retreat so that the Baron's features were somewhat invisible.

Now I know, dear reader you are expecting a description of pure horror. An apparition of a ghoul harvested from dead flesh. But what met my eyes was a man of medium height, with thinning brown hair receded on a pale forehead dressed in a tattered forest green bathrobe, while scuffed black leather slippers adorned his feet. His eyes were beady and his legs bandy.

He reminded me more of a factory worker from the midlands than a creature nightmares are made of. If this was indeed Dr. Frankenstein's creation then Mary Shelly was far from accurate in her depiction of him.

The Baron buried his hands in the pockets of his bathrobe then started down the stairs. "I'm glad you made it. I didn't expect you so soon, or so late."

He stopped at the bottom of the staircase a half smile on his lips. His black eyes were watchful. "You should have waited until morning to come out to the castle. Herman is quite right about things that go bump in the night you know."

I looked to Noel to take the lead. He cleared his throat.

"Of course, Baron, but we are here and are ready and able to start our investigation immediately."

The Baron smirked. "I suppose you're wondering about the object I spoke of in my letter."

"Yes, sir we are curious." I chimed in.

Noel glared at me then his features relaxed. "Yes, Baron. That as well with your knowledge of the region who the potential suspects might be," Noel said.

The Baron smiled. "If I had told you in the letter what to expect you would never have accepted the case." He paused his eyes thoughtful. "Why don't we go into the library? We'll be more comfortable in there. I believe there have been provisions made for our comfort."

I glanced toward the top of the stairs where Herman had disappeared through the door. How had our host made provisions when his manservant had obviously returned to bed?

The Baron turned on his heel and walked toward a door off the foyer. It was closed but as we approached I could make out a polished brass plaque affixed to the door with the words Dr. Frankenstein's library in raised black letters.

The Baron tapped the plaque with his index finger. "For the tourists. Herman conducts tours of the castle in the summer."

The Baron opened the door and held it for Noel and I as we entered. He closed the behind him once we were all inside.

"Since that God awful film last year we have seen a steady growth in the curious and the zealots." He rolled his eyes.

The library was a magnificent homage to the written word for a bibliophile like me. The built in bookcases rose from floor level to the ceiling some twenty feet over our heads.

Noel snuffed out the candles because at the far end of the room interrupting the shelf of books was a floor-to-ceiling stone fireplace complete with a roaring fire. I gazed at the cracking blue, yellow and red flames and felt the chill begin to leave my frigid body.

In front of the fireplace was an antique Chinese silk rug. In the middle of the rug was an octagon-shaped rosewood coffee table surrounded by four leather wing backed chairs.

"What took you so long, darling?" A slender woman wearing a simple navy blue skirt and a white blouse, with dark curls tired in a loose knot that flowed down her left side, rose from one of the wing chairs and smiled warmly. Her pale grey eyes were as warm as the fire.

"I'm sorry, my love." The Baron smiled in kind. "You know me. I had to make my dramatic entrance."

The woman laughed brightly. "I'm sorry, gentleman. My husband can be such a bore."

Noel stepped forward after removing his fedora and took the woman's hand in his then leaned forward and kissed it lightly. "It is an honor, Baroness."

She smiled at him after he let go of her hand and straightened. "I met your father once. It was summer in Geneva…" she paused and looked thoughtful for a second. "Yes. It was the summer of 1894."

1894? She appeared to be no older than thirty. The mystery deepens.

Noel appeared unfazed by this revelation. With a wave of her fine boned hand the Baroness indicated we should sit across from her. The Baron sat in the wing chair next to hers. We took our seats and now faced the Baron and Baroness Frankenstein. Let me tell you, dear reader it was a surreal moment to be sure.

"I'm sorry," Noel, indicated me. "I should introduce Denis Doyle, my fellow agent."

The Baroness looked delighted. "How wonderful! Imagine the son of the author of those mesmerizing tales of Sherlock Holmes in our library." She patted her husband's hand. "Isn't this extraordinary, darling."

"Yes, dear it is indeed. But these gentlemen are here on a mission of grave importance." He paused and his features visibly flushed. "I make it all sound so trivial."

Noel's expression became serious his eyes attentive. "Maybe now's the time to tell us what this is about, Baron."

The Baron sighed and nodded. He sat back heavily in the chair while the Baroness went to a sideboard where a silver tea service sat. She lifted the tray and brought it to the rosewood coffee table where she set it down. Like any good hostess she began to serve tea to each in turn.

The Baron started to tell his tale.

"After the original Baron died he bequeathed this castle, all its possessions, and his title to me, his creation. Since my only name was The Monster I assumed his family name as my own." The Baroness sat down with a cup of tea in her hand just as the Baron gazed at the delicate creature with her high cheekbones, perfect posture and skin the color of alabaster.

"My wife is also the Baron's creation. She is my BFF."

"BFF?" I asked.

A thin smile crossed the Baron's lips. "Bride of Frankenstein Forever."

The expression in his eyes turned cold. "And when I say forever I mean it literally. I assure you eternity is a long time." Silence interrupted only by the crackle of the burning wood in the fireplace filled the room.

Noel edged forward on his chair and took a sip of the fragrant tea. "Please continue."

The Baron's eyes shifted to Noel. "Elizabeth and I could not sire a child though we desperately wanted one. We thought if there were others of our kind then our loneliness would be cured."

"You didn't…" I breathed. Noel shot me a scathing look to silence me.

The Baron shook his head. "Not at first. We tried every medical specialist in the known world." She shook his head sadly. "But it was all for naught until…."

"Until?" Noel looked as if he was about to fall off the edge of his chair he had slid so far forward.

"We turned to the source we knew would help us achieve our dream." The Baron stood and walked to a shelf of tall volumes. "There used to be two volumes of his journal, until volume two went missing several months ago."

He plucked a book off the shelf and carried it with both hands, owing to its considerable size and weight, to the coffee table.

His wife moved the tray to allow sufficient space for the large, thick book. The Baron placed the book on the table with a soft thump and opened it to the first page.

There in ornate handwriting was the evidence that science had indeed triumphed over death. The Baron's tale was confirmed. This was Victor Frankenstein's record of how he had reanimated dead tissue. And these two beings before me were such creations.

Dizziness came over me as I realized I had been conversing with reanimated bodies. Or rather if the legend were true pieces of bodies sewn together and shot through with electrical energy until they came to life. It was too terrible to imagine.

Upon seeing my distress the Baroness leapt to her feet and rushed to my side. She placed a comforting hand on my shoulder. Her brow was wrinkled with concern.

How sweet she is. If only she weren't an undead ghoul. She cast an annoyed look at the Baron her eyes scolded him.

The Baron sighed stood and rested his hand on the mantel over the fireplace. He stared at the fire.

"Please accept my apology, Mr. Doyle. What you think we are and what we truly are very different things. Yes, we are creations but not in the way that Hollywood debacle portrayed us. We are not comprised of sewn together corpses."

His words did not lessen my revulsion of these creatures.

"We were born like you but we died during a cholera epidemic in…" he paused. "Excuse me, the year is unimportant. The important thing is Baron Frankenstein revived us and gave us new life. Eternal life."

"But what about the child?" Noel spoke with fervor in his voice.

"Yes, we did revive a child using the Baron's notes in this journal." He paused and the edges of his eyes sagged. "Then we did it again."

I looked wide-eyed at my colleague. "There are two of them?"

"Boy and girl?" asked Noel. The Baron nodded.

Noel leaned toward me and whispered "Salt and pepper."

I looked at him quizzically. "What?"

"Boy and girl. Salt and pepper. Get it?"

I did but I shrugged my shoulders as if I didn't. Noel frowned at me.

He turned to face the Baron once again. "So what seems to be at the heart of the problem?"

The Baron rolled his eyes. "We're married with monsters."

I looked around nervously. "Where are they now?"

The Baroness Elizabeth Frankenstein patted my shoulder then walked to her chair and sat again. "Bolt and Stitch are missing. We need your help to find them. That's why we decided to hire you."

***

Children of the vat. At least that's what the Baron called them. They were out somewhere in the world, and the only lead we had was a picture of Bolt and Stitch's high school graduating class. The names of the smiling teenagers in the photo were written on the back.

If the teenage son and daughter of the monster were in the picture I was curious what they'd look like. I looked at the smiling youthful faces and did not see any difference between them. They all appeared fully human.

I flipped the picture over the scanned the names. No Frankenstein's, and no one with the colorful names of Bolt or Stitch.

Children of the Monster

The two devilish children had been missing for three months with no word. The local constabulary had refused to look for the monstrous offspring given their origin and that of their parents. The Frankenstein's had written to every detective agency in Europe and America with a please for help. We had been the only ones crazy enough to respond.

Great, Noel, what have you gotten us into?

I gazed at the picture and read the names on the back of the picture in earnest as Noel took notes. I didn't say anything until Noel and I were in the coach headed back into the village.

"I know one of those names."

Noel looked at me in surprise. When I didn't speak his eyes narrowed. "Well, man out with it. Who?"

"Val Koptnik." I looked smug in my conviction.

Noel frowned. "Who is Val Koptnik?"

"Only the richest man in Limberburger. He owns the local cheese fac...tor...y..." My words petered out as I connected the dots in my mind.

Herman smelled of cheese...Koptnik owns the cheese factory.... volume two of the mad doctors journal is missing...

"How do you know any of this, Doyle?"

"I read about it in the Times."

Noel eyes were wide with surprise. "The Times? The Times of London had an article about a Limberburger cheese manufacturer?"

I shook my head. "In the Limberburger Times on the train while you were sleeping."

"Oh. Quite."

I frowned. "What is it?" asked Noel frustrated with my manner.

"We haven't a moment to lose. We must to get to the cheese factory before it's too late."

Noel scoffed. "Cheese factory? Why? Are you hungry?"

I shook my head just as the coach bounced on the pot holed filled country road. My head struck the roof of the carriage with a sharp snap. I winced and rubbed the sore spot on my crown. "No. Owww...I think... I've found the resolution to this case."

I closed my eyes. It was too terrible to contemplate. "And I think what we'll find at that factory is the stuff nightmares are made of."

With one hand still on my wounded head I stood hunched over, so as not to hit the roof of the carriage, and stuck my head out the window. "Driver... take us to the Koptnik Cheese Factory."

***

The carriage driver left us as soon as we arrived at the cheese factory. No doubt the odor was the deciding factor for his hasty departure.

Not that I blame him.

I pulled out my handkerchief and held it over my nose and mouth.

"Cough. I guess you get used to the smell, eh Doyle?" Noel led the way in the darkness toward a door lit by a bare bulb in a steel fixture hung off a metal pole.

Once at the door I tested the knob. It turned easily. I nodded to Noel and opened the door as quietly as possible. The hinges must have been oiled regularly because the door opened without a sound. I felt the tension in my shoulders ease.

Good so far.

I stepped inside first and Noel followed close behind. The door was on a spring because it closed just as softly behind us. The lights inside were of low wattage bathing the interior in a soft glow. Banks of large steel pipes ran side by side the length of the ceiling toward the center of the plant. Ahead of us in the dim light I could see a steel railing and stairs that led to a lower level. I walked toward the railing and waved to Noel to follow.

Once at the railing we were met by a sea of massive vats of bubbling liquids.

The color of the liquid was different in each. Several shades of red, blue, and yellow were represented.

Primary colors...interesting.

A sudden movement at the corner of my eye made me flinch. But my reaction was too slow. A sharp blow to the head and darkness engulfed me.

***

My head throbbed as I regained consciousness. My head swam from the pain that shot across my forehead and down my neck. I tried to move my arms but realized was tied to a chair by thick ropes. To my right sat Noel also secured by ropes to a chair. He was still unconscious.

"How do you feel?"

I looked around me for the source of the voice and saw a figure in the shadows just outside the cone of light from the bulb that hung over our heads.

"Bolt Frankenstein?"

The figure stepped into the light. My jaw dropped. Bolt had to be at least seventy and was probably much older than that. In accordance with the legends chronological age had little to do with the reality of these man made creatures.

"Yes. I'm Bolt." He was dressed in ash-gray coveralls and a matching work shirt.

His hair was snow white and his face narrow with azure intense eyes. "How do you know me?"

"Your parents engaged me and my partner." With a nod of my head that caused me to wince I indicated Noel. "We're Pinkerton detectives."

A woman dressed identically to Bolt whom I assumed to be Stitch stepped from the shadows. "They don't care about us. They only care about their precious book." She cocked one eyebrow at me. "He wants the journal. Not us."

Bolt who until now had his hands buried in the pockets of his coveralls removed his right hand and with a snub nosed nickel-plated revolver.

Oh, oh...I think we're in real trouble. Boy is Noel gonna kill me for getting us killed.

"No, Bolt, put the gun away." Stitch stepped beside her brother and placed her hand on the gun and eased the barrel down. Bolt looked venom at me, but did as she instructed. "We create life we don't take it. We're not like the Baron."

"So it's true?" I was pleased with myself. I had figured it out. If we left here alive, Noel would have to be proud of me.

Stitch nodded. "Yes, we're creating a new race. It was the dream of Victor Frankenstein to create a race of supermen and we're going to make that dream a reality."

"No, daughter you are not." The Baron and Baroness stepped out of the shadows behind us.

Great. I'm surrounded by ageless monsters who are embroiled in a family dispute. This can't be a good thing.

Stitch screamed and Bolt lifted the pistol and a shot rang out. The light over my head went out casting the room into inky darkness.

I heard grunts and yelling then footsteps running. More angry shouts in the distance then silence.

"Hey, Doyle...what's going?" Noel was finally awake.

"I'll fill you in later, Noel. Right now we have to find a way to get untied..."

"I'm not tied."

After Noel managed to find me in the darkness he untied me and after getting lost several times we finally found the room with the massive vats of bubbling liquids and made our way to the staircase.

Once outside and after an hour of walking we were arrived at the Pigs Snout Tavern.

The next day we boarded a train and headed for London and home.

Along the way I explained the events at the cheese factory to Noel and we agreed we would not be getting paid. In fact, Mr. Thomas would very likely fire us both.

Fortunately, Mr. Thomas was in a good mood when we arrived back at the office. A telegram and a wire transfer had arrived ahead of us.

The Baron had not only paid our usual fee in full he had added a twenty percent bonus for what he described as service above and beyond. He wrote he was grateful for the recovery of the journal and his children.

It was hard for me to think of Bolt and Stitch as children given their appearance.

A month after our adventure in Limberburger I received a large envelope with a Limberburger postmark. It was addressed to me personally.

I placed the envelope flat on my cluttered desk. The sound of cars and trucks outside the office window filled the vacant air. I frowned and eased back in my chair my eyes fixed on the envelope. The spring on the pedestal beneath my chair squeaked softly.

Why would they write to me?

I thought about throwing the envelope into the trashcan next to my desk. I ran one hand in smoothing action and realized inside was a photograph.

Curiosity kills the detective.

I sighed and picked the envelope from the desk and tore off one end. The photograph inside was a family portrait of the Frankenstein's. Scrawled across the photograph were the words:

thanks for everything

love, stitch

In the photograph were the Baron and the Baroness looking as I had met them. But Bolt and Stitch appeared to be around eighteen years old. As I'd suspected the children of the monster had been creating new bodies for themselves at the cheese factory and, when they were fully formed, the Baron transferred their old brains into the new bodies.

The Baron must have been unable to find suitable young subjects when he created his children. Now it appeared that situation had been rectified. Monsters create monsters. How many of them roam the earth? Who would ever believe me that Frankenstein's children are making monsters?

Madness. Utter madness.

Dear, reader I'm going to close this case as a crime of teenage rebellion. Monstrous and ancient the Frankenstein kids may be like teenagers everywhere who sometimes sow a few wild oats. But in their case they sow a few wild monsters.

End of Empire

"MAJESTY, THEY ARE AT THE GATES."

Tsar Nicholas the Fifteenth looked away from the laptop screen where he'd been composing a blog entry about recent events. His bloodshot eyes betrayed the fear that had been growing in his belly since the financial collapse two years ago.

His faithful defense minister, Marshall Vladimir Lenin had been at his side since they were together at the Russian military academy when he was a young Tsarevich in training. His father expected, and in fact demanded, he go through the rigorous academy officer training school.

"How long, Vlad?"

Vlad shook his head. Nicky saw the sadness in his eyes. It was a sad day for them all, and most of all for Mother Russia.

"Not more than fifteen minutes my —" His words were cut off by the sound of an explosion in the distance. His forehead wrinkled as if he were in pain. "We're running out of time, sire."

Nicky sighed wearily and nodded. "Ok, my old friend. Is the Tsarina and my son aboard the helicopter?"

"Yes, sire." A muffled explosion followed by a roar of gunfire closer now punctuated his words.

"Thank you. I have one more e-mail to send before the lines are cut. Then I'll head for the roof. You go ahead."

Marshall Lenin opened his mouth to speak but Nicky silenced him with a gesture. The Tsar still ruled and those who still respected the four hundred year old Romanov dynasty would obey his every move. Marshall Lenin was such a man.

Lenin disappeared from the doorway. Nicky heard the slap of his friends leather boots echoing on the marble floor until they gradually receded into the distance then disappeared into silence.

The crackle of the wood in the floor to ceiling stone fireplace in his study was all that remained. For the moment at least the sounds of battle had finally ended.

Nicky turned his attention back to his lap top screen and clicked on the Internet connection. It opened then he clicked on the bookmark list. He scanned the list until he located the name of his e-mail program. He clicked on the name and the password screen appeared.

Once he was in the program he saw he had a list of e-mails from the every major, and some minor, royal heads of state around the planet no doubt promising undying support for Imperial Russia.

Truth was his cousins in Germany, England, France and the Americas were impotent and had been toothless monarchs for decades. They couldn't support anyone never mind Imperial Russia.

In that time the Russian Empire had thrived. Since the victory over Japan in 1904 the empire had steadily expanded its borders and its influence. The defeat of Japan and the occupation of the Asian countries had solidified the Romanov dynasty's future for decades.

His cousins were jealous of his continued unimpeded rule. They had become puppets of their democratic governments that controlled their old empires.

Russia, and by extension he and his family, were targets.

His Secret Police had gathered evidence those same democratic governments were behind the food riots that had thrown Russia into turmoil.

Now he had to do something he never thought he would have to do. He had to run in order to survive. He'd never run from anything or anyone in his life.

Today was turning out to be an ocean of new experiences.

Nicky keyed in the e-mail addresses of his American cousin, King George the Tenth, and copied King William the Fifth of England. He began to type the message.

Dear, Georgie and Willie, I am about to abandon the palace in St. Petersburg for the last time. It is with a heavy heart I must take an unspeakable action to preserve my empire.

My actions today will have dire consequences for the future of the Russian throne. Consequently I implore you, my beloved cousins to reassure your respective governments they must use restraint in these difficult times, and not to take sides in this rebellion against order if lives are to be saved.

I know you are wondering what I mean by these words but by the time you receive this message it will become very clear what I have done.

Remember, cousins I love you as brothers and that my actions are to preserve Russian autonomy not to destroy it. Please urge the politicians to react with caution.

I am your humble servant,

Nicolas, Tsar of Imperial Russia

June 15, 2017

Nicky closed the laptop without exiting the program and hung his head with his eyes closed. He let a single sob escape between his dry his lips.

"Still sending e-mails, Nicolas?" said a throaty woman's voice to his left. He opened his eyes and he looked in the direction of the voice.

In the flickering firelight a woman dressed in forest green and slate-gray camouflage battle fatigues stood in the entryway to the room with an AK47 cradled under one arm. Her black eyes were narrow and her misshapen nose was dirty as were her cheeks and her hands.

Maybe it was camouflage, then again maybe it was just dirt. Regardless, she held herself like someone fully prepared to shoot anyone who stood her path. The palace guard was gone. They had either deserted and joined the rebellion, or they were dead.

Two pineapple type hand grenades were clipped to loops on the front of her bulletproof vest.

Nicky thought about the pistol he kept in his desk drawer across the room. Only there wouldn't be time to get it never mind shoot it before she cut him down.

Is this how it ends? he thought, killed in my own study by a single rebel?

The absolute ruler of the largest empire the world had ever known is killed in his own home by a peasant, a common thug. Maybe history would call her a freedom fighter who killed a tyrant in defense of the homeland. The irony of the situation did not escape him.

He'd read of stranger things in history texts. But it seemed an odd thing to think about when the history involved you personally.

"Yes, I thought just one more to my adoring fans might be worthwhile." He stood and walked to a cart next to his desk where there were four crystal decanters containing the worlds finest liquors.

"Would you join me in a drink?"

The woman smirked and walked further into the room. Like the warrior she was he watched her eyes shift to the corners where the shadows were deepest. If there were any threats in this room this was from where they would come.

Finally her eyes settled on him once again. A tight smile played across her thin lips. She let the barrel of the AK47 dip toward the floor but he knew she could have it on a target within milliseconds and fired quickly after that.

He selected two crystal sniffers then pulled the lid off the ice bucket. The ice in the bucket on the cart had long ago melted to water so he replaced the lid and selected some fine brandy. He pulled out the stopper and poured two fingers of the amber, smoky liquid in each glass. He replaced the stopper then picked up the two glasses, one in each hand. He turned to face the woman and froze.

She had the automatic rifle leveled at his chest and her eyes were hard. He braced himself for the inevitable bullet that would rip his chest to shreds and slice his heart into pieces.

"Are you going to kill the condemned man before he makes his last request?" he said. Rivulets of sweat trickled down his back.

The woman frowned and lowered the gun. "No, I guess not." She walked over to him and grabbed one of the glasses from his hand then moved far enough away that he would be unable to reach her in one step.

Checkmate.

Nicky grinned then lifted the glass to his lips and took a sip. He preferred the brandy with ice but it was still very fine brandy. There was a gentle heat from the liquor on his tongue before he swallowed. He cradled the glass in both hands and moved behind the desk then sat in the ergonomic chair.

The woman downed the brandy in one swallow. "Not bad," she said. "You royal types live pretty good."

He nodded and eased back into the chair. He set the glass on the desk in front of him and placed his hands out of sight beneath the desktop. Carefully and slowly he would open the drawer and get the pistol. Then he'd shoot her in the middle of her forehead and splatter her brains across the room.

"Agnessa."

"Pardon?"

"My name," she said. "It's Agnessa."

"Really? Your name means chaste or holy doesn't it?" He swiveled the chair side to side.

Agnessa's wide mouth formed a grim smile and she turned away from him to scan the study. She moved to a small table where he kept a jade statue of a tiger. A spoil of the war with Japan. The Japanese were still some of the best artisans in the world and they often paid tribute to his benevolent rule with objects 'd art.

"You have some nice things," she said.

100

"Yes, but they belong to the Russian people not me personally."

His words set off something in her because she spun around and raised the rifle. After pulling the slider on the side of the gun accompanied by a ratcheting sound of metal on metal she aimed the barrel at his head. "I recall a speech where you said you were Russia, as if we the people were nothing." Her tone was tight and edged with bitterness.

Unafraid Nicky smiled. If he was meant to die this day then so be it. But Vlad would be back soon to see what was delaying him. He needed to keep her talking if he was meant to see another sunrise.

The only concern he had was her comrades would show up before Vlad did and then it would be over. The only good news was the Tsarevich was safe in the helicopter. His son would one day take his place, as Tsar and the empire would be saved.

Any way you looked at this day the empire would triumph and live on. The longer he stalled this woman the better his and the empires chances were for survival.

The woman lowered the gun to let it hang loose at the side of her leg. Her lips formed a half smile and she moved across the one of the wing chairs in front of the fireplace.

Using one hand she spun the chair so that it faced him behind the desk then sat and sighed. She laid the gun across her lap. He could see now the safety was still engaged.

It dawned on him this meant her orders were to keep him alive. His face cooled as the blood drained away. The rebels didn't want him dead just yet.

A trial. A kangaroo court where he'd be paraded before the world and his so-called crimes against humanity would be exposed for the entire world to see. Then he'd be executed.

It was the perfect plan. All the appearances of legality, the outward appearance of law and order, the allegations, some true, others exaggerated broadly or within a narrow definition set by his enemies. If there was one thing he had plenty of it was enemies. Absolute power generated jealousy in the hearts of some men, and burned holes in their souls they would do anything to plug, even if it meant tearing him and his family down. Even the destruction of a thousand year old empire meant nothing to such men.

More importantly a trial would mean the end of Imperial Russian. Even his son would be unable to set aside the alleged atrocities of the Tsar. Bogdan Alexis Romanov would never be Tsar.

For the first time in his life, Nicky discovered the true meaning of fear. His mouth tasted metallic, lacking even one molecule of moisture.

He wrapped the fingers of one hand around the glass on the desk in front of him. His hand trembled so he hesitated before lifting the glass of brandy to his lips. He raised the glass quickly to his mouth, took a large swallow then slapped it on the desk once again. A trickle of liquor ran from the left side of his mouth. He wiped it away with the back of one hand.

His eyes flitted to his captor. Her dirty features were split by a sardonic grin. "Scared, huh?" she said.

He blew out his cheeks and thought about her question. She was right. He was scared. For the first time he was really scared. What a strange feeling. He thought for a second or two he might vomit but he held himself in check by taking in a slow breath.

"Yes, Agnessa, I am scared," he said finally.

She frowned and shifted her bottom in the tall backed chair. "Why? I thought you were the brave Tsar who defeated the United Arab Empire, and who stormed Beijing to bring the Chinese communists to the peace table. You tamed a country of a billion people." She shook her head, "Now you're afraid of one woman with a gun." She patted the stock of the AK47 and grinned.

"It's not you," he said averting his eyes to stare at the fire.

"Oh?" she said. "What then?"

"A public trial," he admitted.

"A trial?" She chuckled. "Every despot faces their day in court eventually."

"I'd rather face God's wrath than be humiliated before my people and the world."

He heard the scrape of her boots over the tiles when she stood, followed by a metallic click he knew well. She had disengaged the gun's safety.

He kept his eyes locked on the yellow and orange flames that had begun to die down. Soon all that would remain would be a red warm glow. The fire appeared to be friendly. At least something in this room was friendly.

The air seemed to move as she came toward him. It fascinated him how time seemed to slow down as if this were a movie or television show when something terrible was about to happen.

He heard her footsteps as she came up behind him. This was followed by the jab of the gun's muzzle being pressed into the back of the chair. It was an interesting sensation because he never thought he would feel something stuck into the back of the leather chair.

"I'm going to die now, is that it?" he asked.

"Isn't it what you want?" came the reply her voice a low whisper.

He started when there was a gunshot. It didn't seem that loud and there was no pain.

I'm dead, he thought. My world is over. He closed his eyes as tears blurred his vision and streamed down his cheeks.

"Majesty?" said a familiar voice.

His eyes flew open and he swiveled to look at the entryway. He recognized the shape of General Stalin standing in the shadows left behind by the retreating fire. In his right hand was a pistol, a trail of white smoke drifted from the barrel.

The gun stuck in his back had disappeared. His heart jumped when he heard it clatter to the floor.

Nicky shot a glance over his right shoulder and saw Agnessa's face, her eyes wide with surprise. Her brow wrinkled then relaxed as pain began to drift away from her nerve endings.

"General?" she said in a hoarse whisper. "Why?" She took a step back out of his field of vision so Nicky turned in the chair to face her.

The dying woman locked eyes with him. "I'm sorry," she gasped her voice a whisper just before her eyes closed for the last time and she collapsed to her knees then fell forward landing on her face. The automatic rifle lay on the floor beside her where she'd dropped it. Her body trembled and there was an unearthly rattle as the air emptied from her lungs.

Her heart must have still been beating because a pool of dark blood spread outward from beneath her. Finally her body relaxed and he knew she was dead.

At least she knew no more pain. He stood and stepped around the pooling blood.

"Please stay where you are, Majesty," said the General.

"It's okay, General. I'm fine. I have a helicopter to catch."

"No, Majesty, you do not."

Nicky felt anger rise in this throat. He looked at the general and realized the pistol in his hand was leveled at him now. What was this all about?

"General, where is Marshall Lenin?" He had to get this moronic officer back in line and see his family to safety.

"He's dead, sir." The General's brow furrowed and he glared at Nicky. "And so is your family. Sir."

His family? His wife, his son. Dead? His jaw tightened. "What happened?"

"A shoulder launched missile. Sir." General Stalin moved into the room keeping the pistol trained on him. The waning firelight flickered off the medals on his chest. And there were a lot of them. Nicky didn't know Stalin well, but he knew he was a hero of the Russian Empire.

The general had received every decoration the empire offered for heroism, and sacrifice yet he had survived every war of the past twenty years. Most of Russia's long list of heroes eventually died in battle. Somehow Stalin survived.

Nicky's eyes narrowed and his scowled. "Who fired at the helicopter?"

"The woman is dead. Sir," replied Stalin his eyes free of any emotion.

"You killed her didn't you, General?" Stalin nodded. "You're the leader of the rebellion aren't you, General?" Again Stalin nodded.

"And you are going to shoot me aren't you, General?"

Without responding Stalin fired.

The bullet entered Nicky's chest and pierced his heart. The sudden blow knocked him off his feet.

He landed hard on his back and the air rushed from his lungs.

He stared at the thick wooden beams that ran east to west along the ceiling of the study. They looked solid and magnificent.

He blinked.

The immediate pain was more terrible than he imagined but it quickly began to wane as his heart slowed and the blood vessels that supplied life giving blood to his nerves began to sag until the plentiful flow was reduced to a trickle then disappeared all together.

Death wasn't so bad. His son was dead now he was dead. The rebels assassinated much of his family in the past few months. Aunts, uncles, cousins, both immediate and distant, were gone. No doubt, Stalin would ensure all royal blood would be purged from Russia forever.

The empire was truly at an end.

Darkness crept from the edges of his vision. Stalin moved to stand over him. His dark eyes gazed down at him.

"Why?" Nicky managed to gasp.

"To create a new dynasty, naturally," came the reply.

Nicky's lips formed a gentle smile. All hail, Tsar Joseph Stalin the Fir —

Then world of Tsar Nicolas Romanov disappeared into a swirling dark vortex.

About the Author

International selling author, Russ Crossley writes romance under the name R.G. Hart, mystery/suspense under the name R.G. Crossley, and science fiction and fantasy under his own. This year there will be re-issues the romantic comedies, Bachelorette: Zombie Edition by Champagne Books, and Antique Virgin by 53rd Street Publishing, paranormal romantic comedy, Zomopolis, and a new western romance entitled, The Fire In Their Hearts co-authored with R.S. Meger will be published in 2013 by Champagne Books. Also, look for another Aloha adventure, Bloody Betty Queen of the Pirates coming in the spring of 2013 from Champagne Books.

In addition the near future suspense novel, The Last Serial Killer by R.G. Crossley was recently released by 53rd Street Publishing in ebook and trade paperback versions.

He has sold several short stories that have appeared in anthologies from Pocket Books, St. Martins Press, at Smashwords, Amazon, and other e-retail sites.

With his wife, romance author R.S. Meger, he owns and operates a small press publishing company, 53rd Street Publishing. The company began in April 2011 and now has over one hundred e-book titles and a number of print titles, with more planned in 2012 and 2013.

He is a member of SF Canada and the Greater Vancouver Chapter of Romance Writers of America. He is also an alumni of the Oregon Coast Professional Fiction Writers Master Class taught by award winning author/editors, Kristine Katherine Rusch and Dean Wesley Smith.

To find a complete listing of his work check out his website http://www.rghart.com, http://russstory.blogspot.com.Razor's blog can be found at http://razorandedge.blogspot.com

Feel free to contact him on Facebook or Twitter. He loves to hear from readers

Other books by the Author

Titles as R.G. Crossley

Short Stories

Razor and Edge Mysteries
The Kidnapping of Billy Buttons
String of Pearls
Death by Clown
Beggin' For Murder
Ragged Ice
The Grand Central Mystery
A Strange Case of Undead Murder

Jazz Stiletto Mysteries
A Day Without Sunshine
Skullduggery

Non-Series Mysteries
Mirror Image
Dangerous Waters
Cape Disappointment
Boomerang
The Watcher of Wayburn Street
The Apprentice
Drip!
A Beautiful Friendship and The Parrot of Doom
Robine's Diary
The Christmas Club

Loose Ends
Splatter Pattern
It Takes Two

Anthologies
The Adventures of Razor and Edge:
Five Tales From The Quirky Detective Team

Novels
A Bad Case of Loyalty
The Last Serial Killer
Shear Murder

Titles as Russ Crossley

Novels
Attack of the Lushites
Revenge of the Lushites (coming soon)

Short Stories
Countdown
Shoeless Moe
Round Up At The Burger Bar:
The Story of Trixie Pug, Parts 1, 2, 3, 4, 5, 6, 7
Five Minutes
Blossom Queen, Barbarian
The Secret
The Family Line
End of the Flies

With Death You Get the Eggroll
The Penguin Sleeps With The Fishes
Only The Worthy
Hero For A Day
End of Empire
Strange Bedfellows
Big Business
A Perfect Crime
The Wise Guy and The Pirates
In Search of the Perfect Cup
T.I.N. Men
The Legend of G and the Dragonettes
The Incredible Mr. Fix-It
Lock Stock and Barrel
Divided Loyalties
Cave of Wonders
A Family Empire
Until We Meet Again
Dragon Rising

Presents Anthology Series
Tales of Urban Fantasy
Five Tales of Bizarre Detectives
Tales of Mystery and Suspense
Tales of Weird Fantasy
Spies, Detectives, & Heroes
Tales of Twisted Crime
Tales of The Unexpected
Tales From Space
10 by Russ Crossley
Round Up At The Burger Bar: The Story of Trixie Pug,
Parts 1- 5 The Beginning

Worlds of Science Fiction and Fantasy
More Tales of Mystery and Suspense
Ladies of the Jolly Roger
Justice Served

Titles as R.G. Hart

Short Stories
Tikka's Big Day
"My Partner the Zombie" —
Hungry For Your Love Anthology
(St. Martin's Press)
Big Hairy Deal
One Red Shoe
A Bad Day in Lunden Texas
Hook Island
Grind Manor
Bloody Betty, Queen of the Pirates

Anthologies
Love Stories

Novels
Bachelorette: Zombie Edition
Antique Virgin
The Fire In Their Hearts
with R.S. Meger (coming soon from Champagne
Books)
Zomopolis